BETTY A
THE NIGHT
JOGGER

BRYSON ARNOTT

For Isabelle Arnott and Alana Ingram

CONTENTS

CHAPTER 1

THE NIGHT OF THE ATTACK

A young girl named Betty walked merrily down a street in the early evening. She pulled out her violet umbrella and sang *"the one who got the winner becomes that little bell, now my girl is feeling great and knows my truth to tell"*. She kept singing until she flung her umbrella out in front of her, and it pulled her upwards. She flew up high into in the air, the strong wind was giving Betty a head-ache.

She remembered at school her cooking teacher Ms A-lar telling the class "the one who saves the master saves the life of a…" and then she screamed "hazard!". Betty thought about it but did not know what that meant.

Later that evening, she saw a dance competition going on. There was a person named Mackie. She had just met her and said hello when just then there was a loud bang!

Betty jumped towards a wall, picked up a clean paint brush from her pocket, and she brushed it on the wall. Nine days ago Betty's school was attacked. Ms A-lar was mid-sentence when the attacker appeared. That day she used her brush in the corridor and saw the same finger print that she saw just now.

Just then she saw a man and had a sinking feeling that he was going to hurt her. Betty turned super-speed. A blast of wind was going to fall on her with some sparkler bombs! She turned her magic umbrella back into a normal umbrella. Betty covered herself from the big wind that could fall on her and it fell on the attacker instead. He was smashed underneath it but it looked as if he could break free any moment.

Betty saw her parent's house in the distance. She lowered her umbrella and her green pony tails lifted up and started to spin. It was like Betty was swimming. She grabbed her umbrella tightly. There was a double dot at the end of Betty's umbrella. It swooped her up, carried her off, and threw her through her front door.

CHAPTER 2

THE BARKS

Betty lived in the school dormitories but her parents lived in a house nearby. Her classmates called her parents Mr and Mrs Bark. They lived in an old hut and hated going to school because it was a long journey. It was past a river, up a sky-scraper and back down, then following that road for twenty six miles from the Bark's house to the school. Mrs Bark barely had nails. Mr Bark had giant hands. He was also a science teacher.

Mr Bark walked in to the room telling Betty "Don't make your hair into two pony tails, do it in one". Mr Bark was worried because when Betty was two she was doing that swinging thing with her hair and almost broke a finger.

Betty was in an acting competition later that night. She was going to perform in front of every person in town. Mr and Mrs Bark didn't want to leave because the stadium wasn't comfortable like the Bark's house. Mrs Bark was holding a shell and changing Betty's outfit for the acting competition. The outfit did not feel nice. Mr Bark said "practice makes perfect". Then Mrs Bark put a lot more spray into Betty's hair. Betty asked Mrs Bark "why do we need more spray?" Mrs Barks said "because you have to smell nice" Betty said "but no one is going to smell me."

Then Mrs Bark swooped Betty's hair up. It did not feel nice because a needle was in the shell and the needle was tied to Betty's hair. Betty's hair was green but Mr Bark said to Mrs Bark "remember to dye Betty's hair blue soon". Her parents thought her green hair might be causing all the troubles at school lately. Once Betty was dressed and ready all the Barks went outside to wait for the taxi to go to Betty's acting competition.

CHAPTER 3

THE FIRST SCHOOL ATTACK

It was back to school the next day. Betty was in her eighth year. This year at school, learning felt different. Every day school was even better, well at least for Betty. One day Betty heard Ms A-lar talking to Ms Gown the history teacher saying "Ogkak". Betty felt like her ears were popping. She tried to listen as best she could. She only heard one more word of what her teachers were saying. It was "maybe".

Then a man ran down the corridor past them and grabbed Betty's green hair before she could stop him. UFOS were suddenly flying above her! She got sucked into one! She found a way out but needed a key. At last she saw the key, she grabbed it and jumped out. A stone magically appeared in her pocket and when she touched it, it stopped the UFOS in their tracks.

Betty then teleported with her magic umbrella to a coffee shop. A strange man almost put a sword to Betty's neck-almost because Betty teleported again just in time to the cooking class she was late for. Ms A-lar made Betty drink the dreaded crowp juice for being late. It is a food that you drink. It hurts your body and the worst thing is that it gets on your teeth.

Betty tried to relax but it didn't work because Professor A-lar was making an evil face. Betty was still trying to relax when she heard a voice that sounded like Mr Bark's voice in the hall. He was saying "stop stop, just go, wipe it off, I will call the principal now! Mrs Bark call the principal" and they were screaming until it ended.

When Betty opened her eyes her parents had gone, as well as whomever they were talking to. The principal walked into the room and took Betty back to her dormitory.

CHAPTER 4

THE SECRET ROOM

The next morning Betty woke up and just four seconds after she woke up she heard a knock. Betty opened the door and saw a man who had black hair and was very tall. "Betty are you an eighth year or not ?" He said. Betty replied "yes -but but …how do you know my name? and how do you now my room number?" "I know every new eighth year, now come to a place where school is even better" said the man. Betty said "I will try it out", "good" said the man.

Betty and the man were walking down the corridor when the man said "my name is Jace" "Betty Bark" she replied.

When they were just at the lobby Jace stopped. "Do you want the rest of my MG ?" Jace asked "What is a MG?" Said Betty.
The man told her it is a blueberry muffin dipped in a melted dark chocolate.
Betty said "no thank you."

Just then the man called Jace jumped up to a wall and fell through a black spot that appeared on the wall. When Betty went near the giant black spot it was actually a bubbling rock. Betty then jumped through the bubbly oozing rock. Betty realised when Jace fell through the dark space he was just getting sucked into a secret room. Betty heard people talk about secret rooms sometimes at school but had never seen one herself. "Betty hurry up!" shouted Jace.

Jace pulled a letter from his pocket and put it in Betty's pocket. Not wanting to disturb Jace, Betty did not say any thing and just read it silently. It said **go to the top of School Street -been here since 400 BC - there are 500 shops there-** and Jace also wrote **buy the**

Guide of School Lane for 9p and a recorder for 14p. Betty bought all the things on the list. Since it was Betty's first time travelling through the secret room Jace said Betty could also place an order for a hamster, to be delivered next term. Betty picked the only green hamster in the lot, and signed her name before returning back the way she came to her dormitory. The black spot on the wall disappeared behind her.

CHAPTER 5

THE SECOND TO LAST WALK

The next night Betty was walking home. It was a gloomy stormy night. Nine minutes after Betty came out of the school her hair started to spin and she glided up. She could have taken the bus but it was far too risky with this mysterious man about. Betty swam home backstroke. It was hard to do it to all the way home so Betty shook her umbrella and teleported instead.

When Betty got home she saw a giant skull filled with smoke. Next to the skull were people with helmets and on the helmets it said 'the Night Jogger'. Betty let go of her umbrella and it flew towards the skull and broke it. Betty's umbrella swung back to her but the people next to the shattered skull were zooming towards her. Betty managed to stop both of the people with her opened umbrella.

Just then Betty heard a unknown voice softly singing *"ahhhh! my grace and beauty ! ahhhh I'm so lovely! There's no one like me, no one thisssss good "*. Betty walked toward that sound. She walked to it because her ears popped again. You would think Betty knew better after all that had happened in the year.

When Betty arrived to the girl she saw it was a trap. It was actually a blonde skinny pale girl who did not seem to be a good personality to Betty. "I would pick silver hair if I was you" the girl said ominously "do not talk about my hair" said Betty sharply. Then she shut the girl out of her room .

CHAPTER 6

THE TEMPLE

When Betty woke up it was Saturday so she was free from lessons. The first thing in Betty's diary was a walk. When Betty went out she usually only went four miles. She was alone and the Barks would not know if Betty walked up to the strange-smelling forest. From the other end of the forest it was nine miles to get to home.

Betty was walking down a street called Hot-Cross Avenue when she saw the temple entrance. Betty took a picture and then saw a note on the door that said:

4th May 2007

To Mr Tiley

*Dear Mr Tiley I think that today or sometime
soon we will find Betty's school and build in
the dungeon so no one will find us and then I
will be more powerful
from the Night Jogger*

Betty thought this was very strange. She
walked to this temple every two days in the
week but every day in the weekend. There had
never been a note on the door before.

Some time passed and now it was the
second of June. It was nearly the end of Betty's
eighth year. Betty was beginning to wonder if
they would be working in the dungeon so she
was sneaking to the dungeon to check. Luckily
so far they had not started work yet.

One time Betty saw holes on the top of the
front wall. She listened to what the people
inside were talking about. It was something

about that note that Betty saw a long time ago. She felt like there was a battery charging inside of her, preparing for something soon.

CHAPTER 7

THE NIGHT JOGGER

It was time Betty went inside the dungeon. It was foggy, rotten smelling and pitch black. Betty tried to find light but there was not any light. Who would even live in a rotten house? she thought. Just the she found out that people did live here because she heard guards talking about guarding the head master of this building.

Betty spied a sign that said head-master's office to the right. Betty sneaked and climbed at the same time, keeping towards the right. So she would not be bored she imagined what there might be in the head-master's office. Betty looked up and then to the left and then a little bit down and saw the head-master's office. Strangely the head-master was not inside .

Betty ended up near the guard so this part was hard to sneak but finally she reached the head-master's office. A man walked out of a doorway.

He was the man that stole Betty's hair! He was the man that tried to hurt Betty walking at the start of the year! And at the coffee shop!

" I am the Night Jogger" the man said sharply. The Night Jogger then pulled out his umbrella. It was dark red and dark red dust was coming out from it. Betty's umbrella did the same but hers was violet. "Well I will win by 100 points" said the Night Jogger, but then as he stepped toward Betty he suddenly slipped over.

Betty pulled him up with the round tip of her umbrella and then Betty said sharply "YOU WERE MY ENEMY BUT YOU CANNOT BE ANYMORE!". In a flash Betty teleported back to her parent's house for the summer holidays after her eighth year. As she drifted off to sleep that night she wondered what might be waiting for her when she returns to school in just a few short weeks.

Betty's adventures continue in
Betty and the Angels of the Horizon.

ABOUT THE AUTHOR

BRYSON ARNOTT

I was born in America, in the state of Missouri. I was raised in England in the county of Bedfordshire. I am 7 years old and I want to be an author when I grow up.

Fact file:
Favourite number: 3 and 8
Lucky number: 14
Worst fear: dogs
School year : year 2
Favourite class: history

Printed in Great Britain
by Amazon

32790703R00016